TE DEUM LAU

SET TO MUSIC FOR

THREE CHOIRS, ORCHESTRA AND ORGAN

BY

HECTOR BERLIOZ.

EDITED BY G. R. SINCLAIR.

Order No: NOV 072322

NOVELLO PUBLISHING LIMITED
8/9 Frith Street, London W1V 5TZ

CONTENTS.

TE DEUM.

№ 1. TE DEUM.

Hector Berlioz, Op. 22.

f
- - - mus.
Te ve-ne-ra - tur
Te De - um lau - da - mus, te Do-minum con-fi - te - - mur; Te
- - -mus, te De-um lau - da - mus,lau - - da - - mus. Te ve-ne-
ter-ra, te ve-ne-ra-tur om - nis ter - - ra.
om- - -nis ter - ra, te om - - nis
lau-da-mus, te De-um, te lau - -da - mus,
- ra - tur om-nis, om - - - nis ter - - - ra,
Te lau - da - - - - - - - - - - - - -
Te De - -um lau - da - -mus, te Do - minum confi-

B

Nº 2. TIBI OMNES.

C

Nº 3. DIGNARE.

38

12386

44

12386

№ 4. CHRISTE REX GLORIÆ.

46

12886

E

Nº 5. TE ERGO QUÆSUMUS.

-san - - gui-ne re - - de - mis - - ti,

re - - de - mis - - ti. Te er - go quæ - sumus,

hu-mi-li-bus tu - -is fa-mulis sub - -ve-ni.

27

p **1st CHOIR, Soprano.** *dim.*

Fi - at su-per nos mi-se-ri-cor-di - a tu - a, Do - - mi-

2nd CHOIR, Contralto. *dim.*

p Fi - at su-per nos mi-se-ri-cor-di - a tu - a, Do - - mi-

27

p *dim.*

№ 6. JUDEX CREDERIS.

F

40

Nº 7. MARCH.

FOR THE PRESENTATION OF THE COLOURS.

Allegro non troppo. ♩ = 92.

H

Printed and bound in Great Britain by
Caligraving Limited Thetford Norfolk